Panfish Secrets

Mastering Micro-Lures for Lake & Pond Fishing Success

By Richard Coleman

Dedication

For my Father-whose steady hand, Quiet humor, and love
of the outdoors still guide every cast I make.

Richard Coleman

Acknowledgment

Thanks to the friends and fellow fishermen who shared spots, swapped micro-lures, and reminded me that good company matters more than a full stringer and to my family- for never minding the tackle boxes in the kitchen and the mud on the boots.

About the Author

Richard Coleman has spent more than sixty years pursuing his lifelong passion for freshwater fishing throughout New York's ponds, lakes, and rivers. Known to friends and readers as an Angler for Life, he combines old-school knowledge with modern finesse techniques, from micro-lure presentations to light-tackle setups.

Drawing on decades of experience both on the water and in professional life, Richard brings readers a genuine appreciation for the simple joy of casting a line, observing nature, and refining one's skill with every trip outdoors.

Author portrait created using AI illustration based on an original image of the author.

Follow on Amazon:
www.amazon.com/author/richardcoleman

Richard Coleman

Table of Contents

Chapter 1: Why Micro-Lures Work

Most anglers start with the same logic: big bait, big fish. And while that's true in certain situations, when you're targeting panfish like bluegill and crappie -especially in small ponds and lakes – the opposite is often more effective. These fish spend their lives feeding on tiny prey: insects, larvae, zooplankton, minnows no longer than a fingernail. Their diets are built on micro meals. It's no surprise that micro-lures, designed to imitate these small bites, are often the key to success.

Bluegill and crappie are opportunistic feeders. They'll take advantage of whatever is most available in their environment. In shallow ponds, this usually means: insect larvae (mayflies, midges, dragonflies), tiny crustaceans and zooplankton, and small minnows or fry from bass and other panfish. Unlike predator fish that chase larger prey, panfish often 'sip' or 'peck' at tiny targets. This feeding behavior means that standard-size lures can overwhelm or scare them. Micro-lures, in the 1/64 oz to 1/16 oz range, match their natural forage and give you more bites.

One of the most common frustrations pond anglers face is fishing pressure. In public waters - especially easy-to-reach ponds - fish get hooked, released, and re-hooked again. They learn quickly that flashy, oversized lures are dangerous. By switching to micro-lures, you break the pattern. Small presentations look natural, subtle, and safe. They don't trigger alarm bells the way a large spinnerbait might. In fact, many pressured fish that refuse bigger offerings will eagerly bite a 1-inch plastic grub or a 1/80 oz hair jig.

Think of micro-lures as a finesse tool. They don't trigger aggression. They trigger confidence strikes -the fish sees something tiny and edible, and it doesn't take much effort to eat it.

Another reason micro-lures are so effective is their versatility.

With the same ultralight jig head and plastic, you can: fish under a float for suspended crappie, swim slowly along weedlines for bluegill, or let the bait fall like an insect for shallow-feeding fish.

A single tackle tray of micro-lures gives you more flexibility than an entire backpack of large lures.

Micro-lures are designed to be fished on ultralight tackle-rods rated for 2-6 lb line, reels spooled with 2-4 lb mono or 6–8 lb braid. This gear isn't just fun, making even a hand-sized bluegill feel like a trophy, it also maximizes your lure's action. Light line lets tiny jigs sink naturally instead of dragging, sensitive rods detect the faintest tick of a bite, and small reels handle delicate presentations without overpowering.

Using the right setup, you'll hook fish that you'd never even feel on heavy gear.

One of the golden rules of fishing is match the hatch – imitate what fish are naturally eating. Micro-lures make this easy. For example: in spring, tiny black or olive jigs resemble larvae. In summer, small shad-colored plastics mimic minnows. In fall, micro tubes and spinners excel. In winter, sluggish fish prefer slow-moving, subtle baits like tungsten ice jigs tipped with plastics.

A common myth is that micro-lures only catch small fish. In reality, they catch numbers and quality fish. Many trophy crappie and bull bluegill feed primarily on small forage. By downsizing, you increase your hookup rate, and bigger fish are often mixed right in.

Unlike large reservoirs, small waters don't always have a strong population of shad or other big forage species. Food sources are limited and often smaller. Micro-lures mimic what's actually available. That's why they shine in neighborhood ponds, park lakes, farm ponds, and backwater coves of larger lakes.

One of the best parts of micro-lure fishing is its accessibility. You don't need a boat, expensive tackle, or heavy gear. A single ultralight rod, a spool of 4 lb test, and a $10 box of lures is enough to get started. This makes micro-lure fishing perfect for beginners, kids and families, and experienced anglers looking for light-tackle fun.

Micro-lure fishing is about finesse. You'll need to pay attention to the subtle twitch of your line, the way your lure falls through the water, and the tiny tap of a bluegill bite. This kind of fishing demands focus, but it also provides reward. Every catch feels earned. Every strike feels electric. And when you land a trophy fish on a lure no bigger than your thumbnail, you'll know the power of going small.

Micro-lures work because they: match the natural diet of panfish, overcome fishing pressure in small waters, offer versatility in rigging and presentation, pair perfectly with ultralight gear, catch both numbers and trophy fish, fit the food chain of ponds and small lakes, and make fishing accessible to everyone.

By the end of this book, you'll understand not just why micro-lures work, but exactly how to use them to catch more fish, more often, from any pond or small lake you fish.

TIP: When fishing pressured ponds, downsize both your lure AND your line. Switching from 6 lb test to 4 lb or even 2 Ib can make a huge difference in getting bites. Panfish are sensitive to line visibility, especially in clear water.

Notes

Chapter 2: Ultralight Gear Setup

Rod Selection Table:

Feature	Recommendation	Why It Matters
Length	5'6"-7'0"	Short rods = easy to cast in tight spaces. Longer rods = longer casts.
Power	Ultralight	Handles 1/64-1/8 oz lures and 2-6 lb line.
Action	Fast to Moderate-Fast	Sensitive tips for light bites, backbone for hooksets.

Line Comparison Table:

Line Type	Pros	Cons	Best Use
Monofilament	Cheap, floats, forgiving	Less sensitive	Kids, beginners
Fluorocarbon	Invisible, sensitive	More $, memory coils	Clear water, spooky fish
Braid + Leader	Long casts, no stretch	Visible, needs leader	Deeper water, windy days

If micro-lures are the secret to catching more panfish, then ultralight gear is the key to making them work. The right rod, reel, and line don't just make fishing more fun - they bring your tiny lures to life in the water. Without the proper gear, even the best micro-lure will sink awkwardly or fail to draw strikes.

Why Ultralight Gear Matters: Sensitivity - Panfish bites are often subtle - a quick tap, a sideways glide of your line. Ultralight rods let you feel everything. Action - Light rods and line allow micro-lures to move naturally, without drag. Fun factor - A half-pound bluegill feels like a five-pound bass when you're on 2 lb test!

Rod Selection: When choosing a rod, think about length, power, and action.

Reel Selection: Spinning reels are the gold standard for ultralight fishing. Look for sizes 500 to 1000. Smooth drags are critical—panfish can make quick runs, and light line snaps easily without a forgiving drag.

Line Selection: Line is often the most overlooked piece of the ultralight puzzle.

Hooks, Jigs & Terminal Tackle: Micro jig heads: 1/80 oz to 1/16oz. Hooks: #8-#12 for bluegill, #6–#8 for crappie. Floats: Pencil floats or slip bobbers work best.

Essential Accessories: Polarized sunglasses, small tackle bag, minipliers, lightweight landing net.

TIP: When in doubt, go smaller. Panfish have small mouths and can be finicky. A tiny hook with a small bait almost always outperforms oversized gear.

Chapter Wrap-Up: An ultralight setup isn't expensive. You can often get rod/reel combos under $50 that perform well. Attention to rod action, reel drag, and line choice makes all the difference.

Notes

Chapter 3: Rigging Micro-lures

Rigging micro-lures correctly is just as important as choosing the right lure. Because these baits are so small, a poor rig can ruin the action and reduce your chance of hooking fish. In this chapter, we'll look at the best ways to present micro-lures in ponds and lakes, covering jig heads, floats, drop shot rigs, split shot rigs, and even tandem rigs.

Jighead Rigging: The most common and versatile way to fish micro-lures. Use jig heads from 1/80 oz to 1/16 oz. Thread the plastic lure straight onto the hook to ensure balance. Cast and let the lure fall naturally, or retrieve with tiny twitches.

TIP: Always rig your lure straight on the jig hook. Even a slight bend will cause it to spin unnaturally in the water and spook fish.

Float Rigs: A pencil float or slip bobber allows you to suspend a micro-lure at a precise depth. Perfect for crappie that school mid-water or bluegill feeding near vegetation.

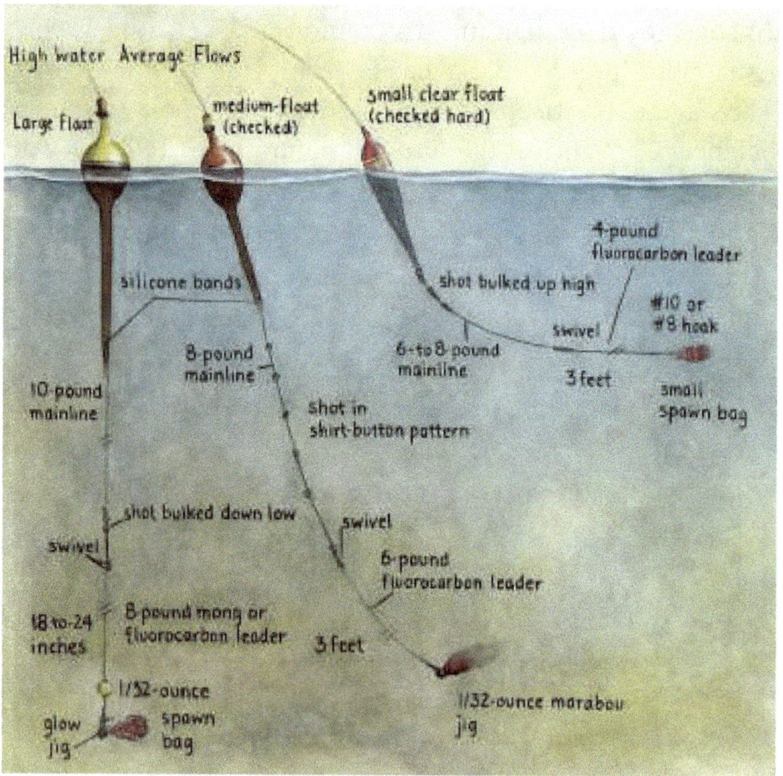

Drop Shot Rigs: Attach a small hook (size 8-12) above a lightweight sinker. Tie the hook with a Palomar knot and leave a tag end for the weight. This rig keeps your micro-lure off the bottom where panfish can see it.

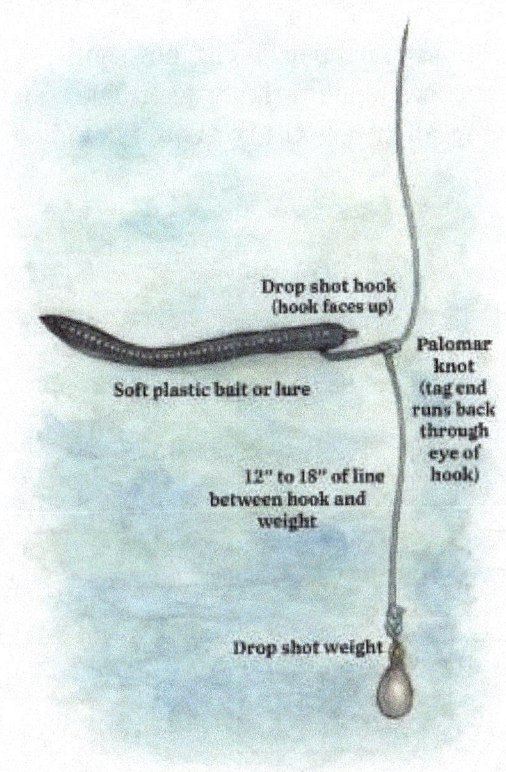

Split Shot Rigs: Place a tiny split shot 12-18 inches above the hook. This gives your micro-lure a slow, natural fall — deadly for finicky bluegill.

Tandem Rigs: Two micro-lures tied in line, one above the other. This can imitate a small school of minnows and often triggers competitive strikes from crappie.

TIP: When tying rigs with light line (2-4 lb), always wet the knot before tightening to prevent friction and line breakage.

Chapter Wrap-Up: Each rig has a time and place. Jigheads are the most universal, floats excel in shallow weedy ponds, drop shots shine in deeper lakes, split shot rigs offer subtle presentations, and tandem rigs trigger aggressive schooling fish. Learning all five will give you a complete micro-lure toolkit.

Notes

____

____

____

____

____

____

____

____

____

____

____

____

Chapter 4: Retrieves & Cadence

Retrieve Comparison Table:

Retrieve Style	Best For	Water Conditions	Notes
Straight Retrieve	Active fish	Warm, clear water	Steady and simple
Stop-and-Go	Bluegill	All seasons	Pause triggers strikes
Twitch	Surface feeders	Shallow, weedy areas	Mimics insects
Lift-and-Fall	Crappie	Mid-depth, cooler water	Great near structure
Dead-Stick	Finicky fish	Cold, pressured water	Patience required

Once you've chosen the right micro-lure and rig, the way you move it in the water determines whether fish strike or ignore it.

This is called retrieve and cadence. In ponds and lakes where panfish feed on tiny prey, subtle movement is everything. In this chapter, we'll cover the most effective retrieves for bluegill and crappie, and when to use each style.

Straight Retrieve: The simplest retrieve. Cast out, let the lure sink, and reel at a steady pace. Works best when fish are actively feeding in warmer water.

Stop-and-Go: Reel a few turns, then pause. The lure sinks or stalls, imitating a dying insect or minnow. Bluegill often strike on the pause.

Twitch Retrieve: Tiny rod-tip twitches cause your micro-lure to dart like an insect on the surface or a fleeing minnow underwater.

Lift-and-Fall: Lift the rod tip to raise the lure, then lower it to let the bait fall naturally. This mimics insect larvae or small baitfish fluttering down. Excellent for crappie holding mid-depth.

Dead-Stick: Sometimes the best retrieve is no retrieve. Let the lure sit still, suspended under a float. Panfish that are suspicious of movement will often inhale a motionless bait.

TIP: Panfish often bite on the pause, not the movement.

Always give your lure a moment to fall or suspend after action.

Cadence Control: Cadence means the rhythm of your retrieve. Fast retrieves excite active fish, while slow, gentle cadences coax wary or cold-water fish. Always experiment: what works one day may fail the next.

Weather and Light Influence: On bright days, panfish may prefer a subtle retrieve. On overcast or windy days, more aggressive movement may be needed.

TIP: Count down your lure after casting. Knowing if fish hit at 3 seconds or 7 seconds tells you the depth they are holding at.

Chapter Wrap-Up: Retrieves and cadence turn a simple lure into a lifelike meal. Practice different speeds and pauses, and always watch your line. The smallest twitch can mean a bite.

Notes

Chapter 5: Fishing Structure & Depth

Depth Zones Table:

Depth Zone	Typical Panfish Behavior	Best Micro-Lure Approach
Shallow (0-3 ft)	Spawning, feeding on insects	Floats, twitch retrieves
Mid-depth (4-8 ft)	Crappie schools, summer shade	Jig heads, lift-and fall
Deep (9-15+ ft)	Winter holding, pressured fish	Drop shot, slow vertical jigs

Finding fish is half the battle. Even with the right lure and perfect retrieve, you won't catch much if you aren't casting where panfish live. In small ponds and lakes, structure and depth are the keys to locating fish.

What is Structure? 'Structure' refers to any physical feature in the water that changes depth, shape, or cover. In ponds and lakes, these include: weedlines and lily pads, brush piles and fallen trees, docks and piers, drop-offs and ledges, and inlets and drains.

Depth Zones: Panfish move up and down in the water column depending on season, weather, and time of day.

Seasonal Structure Use:

Spring - Shallow flats, near weeds and beds.

Summer - Shade from docks, deeper weed edges.

Fall - Roaming near drop-offs following bait.

Winter - Suspended over deeper basins or near brush piles.

TIP: If you can't see fish, cast to edges - where two habitats meet (weeds and open water, shallow and deep) is almost always productive.

Reading a Pond Without Electronics: Not everyone has a fish finder. Luckily, small waters can be read visually: watch for insect hatches or surface dimples (feeding fish), look for water color changes (deeper water is darker), and cast near obvious cover like logs or culverts.

Chapter Wrap-Up: Structure and depth dictate where panfish feed, rest, and spawn. Combine your ultralight gear and micro-lures with smart positioning near cover and edges, and you'll always be fishing in the right place.

Notes

Chapter 6: Seasonal Tactics: Spring Through Winter

Seasonal Summary Table:

Season	Location	Best Lures	Retrieve Style
Spring	Shallow beds, weed edges	Tubes, rubs	Float & deadstick
Summer	Docks, weedlines, shade	Jigheads, topwaters	Lift-and-fall, twitch
Fall	Drop-offs, windy banks	Tandem rigs, spoons	Stop-and-go
Winter	Deep basins, brush	Ice jigs, plastics	Dead-stick, tiny jiggles

Fish don't behave the same way year-round. In small ponds and lakes, temperature swings, daylight, and food sources all change with the seasons. To consistently catch bluegill and crappie, you'll need to adjust your micro-lure approach as the year unfolds.

Spring - Spawning and Shallow Action: Where to Fish – Shallow flats, edges of weed beds, near inlets. Behavior - Bluegill move into 1-3 ft shallows to spawn; crappie gather in schools along shorelines. Best Lures - Small jigs under a float, micro tubes, and grubs in natural colors. Retrieve - Slow and steady or deadsticking under a bobber.

TIP: Look for circular 'beds' in the shallows. Cast beyond the bed and gently retrieve across it.

Summer - Shade and Oxygen: Where to Fish - Under docks, near lily pads, deeper weedlines. Behavior - Panfish seek cooler, oxygen-rich zones in shade or deeper water. Best Lures – Tiny topwaters for morning/evening, jigheads along weed edges during the day. Retrieve - Faster retrieves early/late; mid-day switch to slow lift-and-fall.

Fall - Feeding Frenzy: Where to Fish - Drop-offs, windblown banks, channels leading to deeper water. Behavior - Crappie chase minnows, bluegill feed aggressively before winter. Best Lures - Tandem rigs, micro crankbaits, small spoons. Retrieve - Stop-and-go to mimic baitfish schools.

TIP: Wind-blown shorelines concentrate minnows - fish there first in the fall.

Winter - Slow and Subtle: Where to Fish - Deeper basins, brush piles, near aerators. Behavior - Fish move less, bites are softer, and oxygen levels can affect location. Best Lures - Tungsten ice jigs, small plastics, slow-falling spoons. Retrieve - Almost none – tiny jiggles, long pauses, or dead-stick.

TIP: Use your lightest line in winter - the less resistance, the more bites.

Chapter Wrap-Up: Seasonal changes in pond and lake fishing are predictable if you know what to look for. Fish adapt to water temperature, light, and forage. By matching your lure choice and retrieve to each season, you'll always stay one step ahead of the fish.

Notes

Chapter 7: Weather Swings & Water Clarity

Weather & Water Clarity Effects Table:

Condition	Fish Behavior	Best Lures	Retrieve Style
Sunny	Hold to shade or deeper water	Natural colors, small plastics	Slow, finesse
Cloudy	Roam freely, more active	Bright plastics, spoons	Stop-and-go, twitch
Windy	Push toward wind-blown banks	Tandem rigs, minnows	Aggressive, erratic
Light Rain	Surface feeding, insect activity	Floats, surface lures	Gentle twitch
Muddy Water	Reduced visibility, cautious	Chartreuse, orange, vibration lures	Slow and steady

Weather and water clarity are two of the most important but often overlooked factors in fishing small ponds and lakes. Unlike large reservoirs, small bodies of water react quickly to weather changes, and fish behavior can shift within hours. Understanding how light, wind, rain, and water clarity affect panfish will help you make the right micro-lure choice every trip.

Sunny Days: Bright sun pushes panfish into shade or deeper water.

On clear days, use subtle colors (natural greens, browns, or translucent lures) and longer leaders. Fish near docks, weeds, or deeper edges.

Cloudy Days: Overcast skies spread light evenly through the water, making panfish roam more freely. This is one of the best times for active retrieves and brighter-colored lures that stand out.

Windy Conditions: Wind stirs up food and pushes minnows toward wind-blown banks. Fish those shorelines with stop-and-go retrieves or tandem rigs. Be prepared for more aggressive bites.

Rain: Light rain can improve fishing by cooling the surface and knocking insects into the water. Heavy rain or runoff, however, muddies the water and reduces visibility. Switch to darker lures or those with vibration in stained conditions.

Water Clarity: Clear water requires finesse - light line, natural colors, and slow retrieves. Stained or muddy water allows for brighter colors, larger profiles, and sometimes faster presentations.

TIP: Match your lure color to water clarity. In clear water, think 'match the hatch' with subtle hues. In murky water, use bold colors like chartreuse, orange, or white to get noticed.

Weather Swings: Small ponds can change temperature or clarity within a single day. After storms, fish may move shallow or suspend near inlets. Always adjust quickly - yesterday's pattern may not work today.

Chapter Wrap-Up: By paying attention to light, wind, rain, and water clarity, you can stay ahead of changing fish behavior. Micro-lures give you the flexibility to adjust size, color, and retrieve so that panfish see your bait as the easiest meal available.

Notes

Chapter 8: Troubleshooting No-Bite Days & Common Problems

Troubleshooting Table:

Problem	Likely Cause	Adjustment
No bites at all	Fish not interested	Change retrieve style or speed
Short strikes	Lure too big or hook too large	Downsize lure or hook
Line visible	Clear water, wary fish	Use lighter line or fluorocarbon leader
Snags	Fishing too deep in cover	Use float rigs or weedless hooks
Can't find depth	Fish suspended midwater	Count down or use slip float
Weather shifts	Fish reposition quickly	Adjust depth, color, and speed

Every angler faces days when fish just won't bite. Even in well-stocked ponds and reliable lakes, conditions or small mistakes can shut down the action. Troubleshooting your approach with micro-lures involves changing one factor at a time until you find what works.

Problem 1: Fish are present but ignoring your lure.

Solution- Change retrieve speed, pause more often, or switch to a different retrieve style such as stop-and-go or lift-and-fall.

Problem 2: Short strikes or missed bites.

Solution- Downsize your lure, use a smaller hook, or sharpen your hooks. Sometimes adding a small piece of live bait (like a worm tip) increases hookup rates.

Problem 3: Line visibility spooking fish.

Solution- Drop down to lighter line (2-4 1b) or add a fluorocarbon leader. In very clear water, use natural colors and finesse retrieves.

Problem 4: Constant snags in weeds or brush.

Solution- Use weed-less jig heads, float rigs, or keep your lure just above structure instead of dragging through it.

Problem 5: Fish are suspended at unknown depth.

Solution- Count down your lure after each cast until you find the strike zone. Alternatively, use a slip float to set different depths easily.

Problem 6: Sudden weather changes.

Solution- Adjust quickly. After a cold front, fish may move deeper and prefer slower presentations. After rain, fish may feed near inlets.

TIP: Change only one factor at a time - lure size, color, depth, or retrieve. If you change everything at once, you won't know what actually solved the problem.

Chapter Wrap-Up: Tough days happen, but with patience and adjustments, you can usually turn no-bite days into steady action.

Micro-lures give you flexibility - small tweaks in rigging, presentation, or color can make all the difference.

Notes

____

____

____

____

____

____

____

____

____

____

____

____

Chapter 9: Legal & Etiquette Notes for Stocked Waters

Common Regulations & Etiquette Table:

Rule/Practice	Why It Matters	Angler Responsibility
Licensing	Funds fish stocking and conservation	Carry a valid license
Bag/Size Limits	Prevents overharvest	Follow posted signs
Seasonal Closures	Protects pawning fish	Check stocking schedules
Catch-and-Release	Ensures fish survival	Handle fish gently, use barbless hooks
Sharing Space	Creates fair experience	Give others room, avoid crossing lines
Leave No Trace	Keeps waters clean	Pack out trash, respect vegetation

Fishing in stocked ponds and lakes is not just about catching fish—it's also about respecting the rules and other anglers. Many small waters are managed by local parks, municipalities, or private landowners who set regulations to protect fish populations and ensure a fair experience.

Licensing and Permits: Always check whether a fishing license is required, even for small public ponds. Some areas require additional permits for stocked trout waters or special access ponds.

Size and Bag Limits: Many stocked waters have specific harvest limits. Pay close attention to posted signs about how many fish you may keep and the minimum sizes.

Seasons and Stocking Schedules: Certain ponds are stocked only during spring or fall, and some have seasonal closures to protect fish during spawning. Knowing the schedule can improve your success and keep you compliant.

Catch-and-Release Etiquette: If you plan to release fish, handle them with care. Use wet hands, unhook gently, and return the fish quickly to the water. Barbless hooks make catch-and-release much easier.

Sharing Space: Small ponds often attract many anglers.

Be courteous: don't crowd others, give casting room, and avoid wading through someone else's spot.

TIP: When fishing a crowded pond, keep your casts controlled and lines short to prevent tangles with nearby anglers.

Private Waters: Some farm ponds or private lakes allow fishing by invitation or fee. Always ask permission and follow any rules given by the owner.

Leave No Trace: Pack out all trash, avoid damaging vegetation, and leave the area cleaner than you found it. Respecting the environment ensures continued access for everyone.

Chapter Wrap-Up: Following the law and practicing good etiquette keeps fishing enjoyable for everyone. By respecting limits, sharing space, and caring for fish and the environment, you'll help protect these waters for future generations.

Notes

Chapter 10: Cheat Sheets & Log Pages

One of the most effective ways to improve as an angler is to track what works and what doesn't. By keeping notes on conditions, lures, retrieves, and results, you create a personal playbook that will guide future trips. This chapter provides quick-reference cheat sheets and log templates designed for pond and lake fishing with micro-lures.

Cheat Sheet: Lure Selection by Condition

Clear water - Use natural colors like green, silver, or translucent. Light line (2-4 lb) and finesse retrieves.

Stained water - Bright colors like chartreuse, orange, or white. Add vibration or flash to stand out.

Cold water - Slow retrieves, dead-stick, or lift-and-fall with tungsten jigs or plastics.

Warm water - Faster retrieves, twitch or stop-and-go. Try micro crankbaits or surface lures at dawn/dusk.

TIP: Keep a small waterproof notepad in your tackle bag. Jotting quick notes right after a catch will help you remember details later.

Cheat Sheet: Depth & Structure

Shallow flats - Best in spring for spawning bluegill and crappie. Use floats and small plastics.

Weedlines - Summer and early fall, twitch retrieves with jigheads.

Drop-offs - Crappie school along edges. Use lift-and-fall retrieves.

Deep basins - Winter holding areas. Dead-stick or tiny jiggle retrieves.

Use your Bonus Micro-Lure Fishing Logbook that begins on Page 58.

Chapter Wrap-Up: Cheat sheets and logs turn every trip into a learning opportunity. Over time, your notes will reveal patterns - which ponds produce best in certain seasons, which lures work in specific conditions, and how weather influences panfish behavior. This personal data will become your most valuable fishing guide.

Notes

Appendix A – Knots for Micro-Lures

Strong, reliable knots are essential for ultralight fishing. Because micro-lures are so small, knot choice can affect lure action as well as strength. Below are three key knots every angler should know.

Palomar Knot: One of the strongest and easiest fishing knots. Ideal for light line and small hooks.

Steps:

1. Double about 6 inches of line and pass through the hook eye.

2. Tie a simple overhand knot with the doubled line.

3. Pass the hook or lure through the loop.

4. Moisten the line and pull tight.

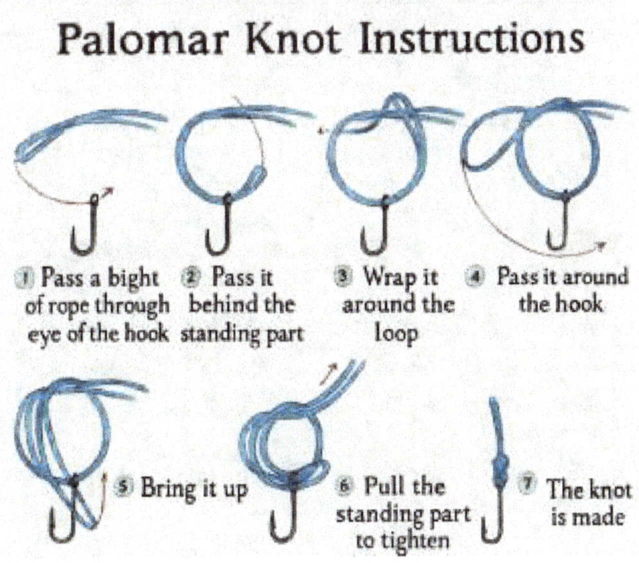

Loop Knot: Gives small lures more freedom of movement. Great for micro crankbaits or jigs.

Steps:

1. Tie an overhand knot in the line, 10 inches above the tag end.

2. Pass the tag end through the hook eye.

3. Bring the tag end back through the overhand knot.

4. Wrap the tag end around the standing line 3-4 times.

5. Pass the tag end back through the overhand knot and tighten.

Improved Clinch Knot: A classic knot for tying small hooks and jigs. Reliable and simple.

Steps:

1. Thread the line through the hook eye and wrap around the standing line 5-7 times.

2. Pass the tag end through the small loop above the hook eye.

3. Then pass it back through the big loop created.

4. Moisten and tighten down securely.

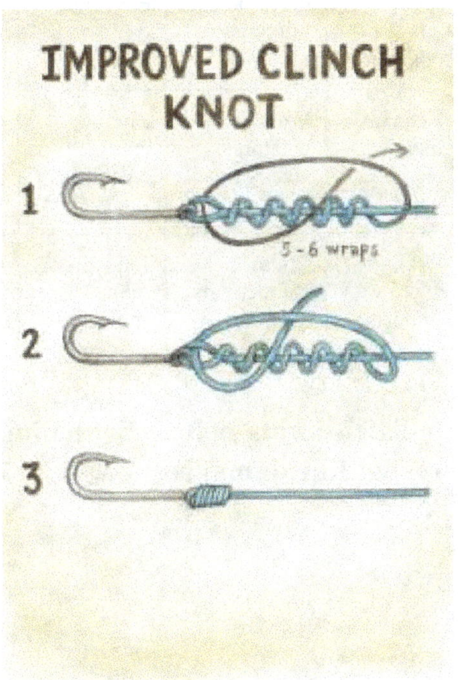

Quick-Reference Micro Lure Table - Northeast Seasons

Species	Spring	Summer	Fall	Winter
Bluegill/ Panfish	Micro jigs, 1" grubs, spinners	Tiny topwaters, beetle spins	Micro spoons, wax worm jigs	Tungsten jigs, tiny plastics
Crappie	Micro tubes, hair jigs, paddletail	Swimbaits, Micro crankbait s	Paddletails, marabou jigs	Glow jigs, micro spoons
Perch	Micro spoons, marabou jigs	Crankbait drop shot minnows	Spoons, drop shot rigs	Jigging spoons, bait-tipped jigs
Bass (Largemouth)	Ned rigs, finesse worms	Weedless creatures, wacky rigs	Micro cranks, creatures, finesse jigs	Rare – finesse worms (drop shot)
Pickerel	Jerkbaits, micro spinners	Micro spinnerbaits, topwaters	Jerkbaits, inline spinners	Occasionally spoons (ice)

TIP: Always moisten knots before tightening to reduce friction and prevent line damage.

Appendix B – Quick Gear Checklist

Before heading out to the pond or lake, it helps to have a simple checklist to make sure you don't forget essential gear. This appendix provides a quick reference list of recommended items for micro-lure and ultralight fishing.

Rods & Reels

- ☐ Ultralight spinning rod (4-6 ft)
- ☐ Spinning reel (size 500-1000)
- ☐ Spare spooled reel (optional)

Line

- ☐ 2-4 lb monofilament or fluorocarbon
- ☐ Optional: 6-8 lb braided line with fluorocarbon leader
- ☐ Spare spool of line

Terminal Tackle

- ☐ Micro jig heads (1/80 to 1/16 oz)
- ☐ Small hooks (sizes 8-12)
- ☐ Floats (pencil and slip bobbers)
- ☐ Split shot weights
- ☐ Swivels and snaps

Lures

- ☐ Micro tubes
- ☐ Small grubs
- ☐ Mini crankbaits
- ☐ Tiny spoons
- ☐ Tandem rig setups

Tools & Accessories

- ☐ Polarized sunglasses
- ☐ Needle-nose pliers or hemostats
- ☐ Line clippers or scissors
- ☐ Tackle box or shoulder bag
- ☐ Small landing net (optional)

Comfort & Safety

- ☐ Fishing license (if required)
- ☐ Bug spray
- ☐ Water/snacks
- ☐ Hat and sunscreen
- ☐ First-aid kit
- ☐ Rain gear (if needed)

Notes

____

____

____

____

____

____

____

____

____

____

Glossary

Cadence - The rhythm or speed of a lure's retrieve.

Catch-and-release - The practice of releasing fish unharmed after capture.

Dead-stick - Fishing technique where the lure is left motionless.

Drop-off - A sudden change from shallow to deeper water.

Finesse fishing - Subtle presentations using light line and small lures.

Jighead - A weighted hook designed to hold soft plastic lures.

Micro-lure - Very small artificial bait designed for panfish and other small species.

Palomar Knot - A strong knot for attaching hooks or lures to light line.

Panfish - A group of small freshwater fish including bluegill, sunfish, and crappie.

Slip float - A bobber that slides freely on the line, allowing adjustable depth.

Structure - Features such as weeds, logs, docks, or depth changes that attract fish.

Bonus Micro-Lure Logbook: Track Your Panfish & Bass Fishing Adventures

This Micro-Lure Fishing Log book is designed to help you keep detailed records of panfish caught, fishing trip details, types of micro-lures used, and for each panfish the presentation, weather conditions, water clarity, etc.

You will determine what works and doesn't in the and doesn't in at the specific lake or pond fished

Micro-Lure Essentials & Pro Tips

- Match your lure size to the forage-tiny baitfish, insects, or small crustaceans.
- Light line increases sensitivity and bite detection.
- Use slow, steady retrieves for pressured fish.
- Experiment with colors-natural tones on clear days, bright hues in stained water.
- Keep hooks sharp and replace split rings when corroded.
- Observe the water: clarity, vegetation, and structure dictate success.

Gear Checklist

Rods (Ultralight/Light)

Reels (1000-2000 size spinning or BFS baitcasters)

Lines (2-6 lb mono or fluoro/8-10 lb braid)

Micro Jigs & Soft Plastics

Inline Spinners & Micro Cranks

Small Floats & Split Shot

Tools: Pliers, Clippers, Scale, Net

Storage Box & Measuring Tape

Seasonal Micro Lure Guide

SPRING - Tiny jerkbaits, micro tubes, small swimbaits

SUMMER - Wacky rigs, topwater poppers, small cranks

FALL - Ned rigs, downsized spinnerbaits, micro jigs

WINTER - Slow finesse plastics, ice micro spoons

Fishing Log #1

Date:

Time:

Weather:

Location/Pond:

Lure Used:

Color/ Size:

Presentation (Wacky, Ned, Texas, etc.):

Line Type & Weight:

Rod/ Reel:

Fish Caught (Species / Size / Qty):

Water Clarity:______ Depth______Temp________

Notes Observations:

____
____
____
____
____
____
____
____
____
____
____
____
____

Fishing Log #2

Date:

Time:

Weather:

Location/Pond:

Lure Used:

Color/ Size:

Presentation (Wacky, Ned, Texas, etc.):

Line Type & Weight:

Rod/ Reel:

Fish Caught (Species / Size / Qty):

Water Clarity:______ Depth_____Temp_______

Notes Observations:

____
____
____
____
____
____
____
____
____
____
____
____
____
____

Fishing Log #3

Date:

Time:

Weather:

Location/Pond:

Lure Used:

Color/ Size:

Presentation (Wacky, Ned, Texas, etc.):

Line Type & Weight:

Rod/ Reel:

Fish Caught (Species / Size / Qty):

Water Clarity:______ Depth______Temp________

Notes Observations:

____
____
____
____
____
____
____
____
____
____
____
____
____

Fishing Log #4

Date:

Time:

Weather:

Location/Pond:

Lure Used:

Color/ Size:

Presentation (Wacky, Ned, Texas, etc.):

Line Type & Weight:

Rod/ Reel:

Fish Caught (Species / Size / Qty):

Water Clarity:_____ Depth_____Temp_______

Notes Observations:

____

____

____

____

____

____

____

____

____

____

____

____

____

Fishing Log #5

Date:

Time:

Weather:

Location/Pond:

Lure Used:

Color/ Size:

Presentation (Wacky, Ned, Texas, etc.):

Line Type & Weight:

Rod/ Reel:

Fish Caught (Species / Size / Qty):

Water Clarity:_______ Depth______Temp________

Notes Observations:

____
____
____
____
____
____
____
____
____
____
____
____

Fishing Log #6

Date:

Time:

Weather:

Location/Pond:

Lure Used:

Color/ Size:

Presentation (Wacky, Ned, Texas, etc.):

Line Type & Weight:

Rod/ Reel:

Fish Caught (Species / Size / Qty):

Water Clarity:______ Depth______Temp________

Notes Observations:

____
____
____
____
____
____
____
____
____
____
____
____
____
____

Fishing Log #7

Date:

Time:

Weather:

Location/Pond:

Lure Used:

Color/ Size:

Presentation (Wacky, Ned, Texas, etc.):

Line Type & Weight:

Rod/ Reel:

Fish Caught (Species / Size / Qty):

Water Clarity:______ Depth______Temp________

Notes Observations:

____
____
____
____
____
____
____
____
____
____
____
____

Fishing Log #8

Date:

Time:

Weather:

Location/Pond:

Lure Used:

Color/ Size:

Presentation (Wacky, Ned, Texas, etc.):

Line Type & Weight:

Rod/ Reel:

Fish Caught (Species / Size / Qty):

Water Clarity:______ Depth______Temp________

Notes Observations:

____
____
____
____
____
____
____
____
____
____
____
____
____

Fishing Log #9

Date:

Time:

Weather:

Location/Pond:

Lure Used:

Color/ Size:

Presentation (Wacky, Ned, Texas, etc.):

Line Type & Weight:

Rod/ Reel:

Fish Caught (Species / Size / Qty):

Water Clarity:______ Depth______Temp________

Notes Observations:

____

____

____

____

____

____

____

____

____

____

____

____

Fishing Log #10

Date:

Time:

Weather:

Location/Pond:

Lure Used:

Color/ Size:

Presentation (Wacky, Ned, Texas, etc.):

Line Type & Weight:

Rod/ Reel:

Fish Caught (Species / Size / Qty):

Water Clarity:_______ Depth______Temp________

Notes Observations:

____

____

____

____

____

____

____

____

____

____

____

____

____

Fishing Log #11

Date:

Time:

Weather:

Location/Pond:

Lure Used:

Color/ Size:

Presentation (Wacky, Ned, Texas, etc.):

Line Type & Weight:

Rod/ Reel:

Fish Caught (Species / Size / Qty):

Water Clarity:______ Depth______Temp________

Notes Observations:

____
____
____
____
____
____
____
____
____
____
____
____
____

Fishing Log #12

Date:

Time:

Weather:

Location/Pond:

Lure Used:

Color/ Size:

Presentation (Wacky, Ned, Texas, etc.):

Line Type & Weight:

Rod/ Reel:

Fish Caught (Species / Size / Qty):

Water Clarity:______ Depth______Temp________

Notes Observations:

Fishing Log #13

Date:

Time:

Weather:

Location/Pond:

Lure Used:

Color/ Size:

Presentation (Wacky, Ned, Texas, etc.):

Line Type & Weight:

Rod/ Reel:

Fish Caught (Species / Size / Qty):

Water Clarity:_______ Depth______Temp________

Notes Observations:

____
____
____
____
____
____
____
____
____
____
____
____

Fishing Log #14

Date:

Time:

Weather:

Location/Pond:

Lure Used:

Color/ Size:

Presentation (Wacky, Ned, Texas, etc.):

Line Type & Weight:

Rod/ Reel:

Fish Caught (Species / Size / Qty):

Water Clarity:______ Depth______Temp________

Notes Observations:

____
____
____
____
____
____
____
____
____
____
____
____
____

Fishing Log #15

Date:

Time:

Weather:

Location/Pond:

Lure Used:

Color/ Size:

Presentation (Wacky, Ned, Texas, etc.):

Line Type & Weight:

Rod/ Reel:

Fish Caught (Species / Size / Qty):

Water Clarity:______ Depth______Temp________

Notes Observations:

____

____

____

____

____

____

____

____

____

____

____

____

____

Fishing Log #16

Date:

Time:

Weather:

Location/Pond:

Lure Used:

Color/ Size:

Presentation (Wacky, Ned, Texas, etc.):

Line Type & Weight:

Rod/ Reel:

Fish Caught (Species / Size / Qty):

Water Clarity:______ Depth______Temp________

Notes Observations:

____
____
____
____
____
____
____
____
____
____
____
____
____

Fishing Log #17

Date:

Time:

Weather:

Location/Pond:

Lure Used:

Color/ Size:

Presentation (Wacky, Ned, Texas, etc.):

Line Type & Weight:

Rod/ Reel:

Fish Caught (Species / Size / Qty):

Water Clarity:______ Depth______Temp________

Notes Observations:

____
____
____
____
____
____
____
____
____
____
____
____
____
____

Fishing Log #18

Date:

Time:

Weather:

Location/Pond:

Lure Used:

Color/ Size:

Presentation (Wacky, Ned, Texas, etc.):

Line Type & Weight:

Rod/ Reel:

Fish Caught (Species / Size / Qty):

Water Clarity:______ Depth______Temp________

Notes Observations:

____
____
____
____
____
____
____
____
____
____
____
____
____

Fishing Log #19

Date:

Time:

Weather:

Location/Pond:

Lure Used:

Color/ Size:

Presentation (Wacky, Ned, Texas, etc.):

Line Type & Weight:

Rod/ Reel:

Fish Caught (Species / Size / Qty):

Water Clarity:______ Depth______Temp________

Notes Observations:

____

____

____

____

____

____

____

____

____

____

____

____

____

Fishing Log #20

Date:

Time:

Weather:

Location/Pond:

Lure Used:

Color/ Size:

Presentation (Wacky, Ned, Texas, etc.):

Line Type & Weight:

Rod/ Reel:

Fish Caught (Species / Size / Qty):

Water Clarity:______ Depth______Temp________

Notes Observations:

____

____

____

____

____

____

____

____

____

____

____

____

____

Fishing Log #21

Date:

Time:

Weather:

Location/Pond:

Lure Used:

Color/ Size:

Presentation (Wacky, Ned, Texas, etc.):

Line Type & Weight:

Rod/ Reel:

Fish Caught (Species / Size / Qty):

Water Clarity:_____ Depth_____Temp________

Notes Observations:

____
____
____
____
____
____
____
____
____
____
____
____

Fishing Log #22

Date:

Time:

Weather:

Location/Pond:

Lure Used:

Color/ Size:

Presentation (Wacky, Ned, Texas, etc.):

Line Type & Weight:

Rod/ Reel:

Fish Caught (Species / Size / Qty):

Water Clarity:_______ Depth______Temp_________

Notes Observations:

____

____

____

____

____

____

____

____

____

____

____

____

____

Fishing Log #23

Date:

Time:

Weather:

Location/Pond:

Lure Used:

Color/ Size:

Presentation (Wacky, Ned, Texas, etc.):

Line Type & Weight:

Rod/ Reel:

Fish Caught (Species / Size / Qty):

Water Clarity:_______ Depth______Temp________

Notes Observations:

____
____
____
____
____
____
____
____
____
____
____
____
____

Fishing Log #24

Date:

Time:

Weather:

Location/Pond:

Lure Used:

Color/ Size:

Presentation (Wacky, Ned, Texas, etc.):

Line Type & Weight:

Rod/ Reel:

Fish Caught (Species / Size / Qty):

Water Clarity:______ Depth______Temp________

Notes Observations:

____

____

____

____

____

____

____

____

____

____

____

____

____

Fishing Log #25

Date:

Time:

Weather:

Location/Pond:

Lure Used:

Color/ Size:

Presentation (Wacky, Ned, Texas, etc.):

Line Type & Weight:

Rod/ Reel:

Fish Caught (Species / Size / Qty):

Water Clarity:_____ Depth_____Temp_______

Notes Observations:

____
____
____
____
____
____
____
____
____
____
____
____
____

Fishing Log #26

Date:

Time:

Weather:

Location/Pond:

Lure Used:

Color/ Size:

Presentation (Wacky, Ned, Texas, etc.):

Line Type & Weight:

Rod/ Reel:

Fish Caught (Species / Size / Qty):

Water Clarity:______ Depth______Temp________

Notes Observations:

____
____
____
____
____
____
____
____
____
____
____
____
____
____

Fishing Log #27

Date:

Time:

Weather:

Location/Pond:

Lure Used:

Color/ Size:

Presentation (Wacky, Ned, Texas, etc.):

Line Type & Weight:

Rod/ Reel:

Fish Caught (Species / Size / Qty):

Water Clarity:______ Depth______Temp________

Notes Observations:

____
____
____
____
____
____
____
____
____
____
____
____
____

Fishing Log #28

Date:

Time:

Weather:

Location/Pond:

Lure Used:

Color/ Size:

Presentation (Wacky, Ned, Texas, etc.):

Line Type & Weight:

Rod/ Reel:

Fish Caught (Species / Size / Qty):

Water Clarity:______ Depth______Temp________

Notes Observations:

____
____
____
____
____
____
____
____
____
____
____
____
____

Fishing Log #29

Date:

Time:

Weather:

Location/Pond:

Lure Used:

Color/ Size:

Presentation (Wacky, Ned, Texas, etc.):

Line Type & Weight:

Rod/ Reel:

Fish Caught (Species / Size / Qty):

Water Clarity:______ Depth______Temp________

Notes Observations:

____
____
____
____
____
____
____
____
____
____
____
____
____
____

Fishing Log #30

Date:

Time:

Weather:

Location/Pond:

Lure Used:

Color/ Size:

Presentation (Wacky, Ned, Texas, etc.):

Line Type & Weight:

Rod/ Reel:

Fish Caught (Species / Size / Qty):

Water Clarity:______ Depth______Temp________

Notes Observations:

____
____
____
____
____
____
____
____
____
____
____
____
____
____

Fishing Log #31

Date:

Time:

Weather:

Location/Pond:

Lure Used:

Color/ Size:

Presentation (Wacky, Ned, Texas, etc.):

Line Type & Weight:

Rod/ Reel:

Fish Caught (Species / Size / Qty):

Water Clarity:_____ Depth_____Temp_______

Notes Observations:

____

____

____

____

____

____

____

____

____

____

____

____

Fishing Log #32

Date:

Time:

Weather:

Location/Pond:

Lure Used:

Color/ Size:

Presentation (Wacky, Ned, Texas, etc.):

Line Type & Weight:

Rod/ Reel:

Fish Caught (Species / Size / Qty):

Water Clarity:_____ Depth_____Temp_______

Notes Observations:

____
____
____
____
____
____
____
____
____
____
____
____
____

Fishing Log #33

Date:

Time:

Weather:

Location/Pond:

Lure Used:

Color/ Size:

Presentation (Wacky, Ned, Texas, etc.):

Line Type & Weight:

Rod/ Reel:

Fish Caught (Species / Size / Qty):

Water Clarity:_____ Depth_____Temp_______

Notes Observations:

____

____

____

____

____

____

____

____

____

____

____

____

Fishing Log #34

Date:

Time:

Weather:

Location/Pond:

Lure Used:

Color/ Size:

Presentation (Wacky, Ned, Texas, etc.):

Line Type & Weight:

Rod/ Reel:

Fish Caught (Species / Size / Qty):

Water Clarity:______ Depth______Temp________

Notes Observations:

____
____
____
____
____
____
____
____
____
____
____
____
____

Fishing Log #35

Date:

Time:

Weather:

Location/Pond:

Lure Used:

Color/ Size:

Presentation (Wacky, Ned, Texas, etc.):

Line Type & Weight:

Rod/ Reel:

Fish Caught (Species / Size / Qty):

Water Clarity:______ Depth_____Temp________

Notes Observations:

____
____
____
____
____
____
____
____
____
____
____
____
____

Fishing Log #36

Date:

Time:

Weather:

Location/Pond:

Lure Used:

Color/ Size:

Presentation (Wacky, Ned, Texas, etc.):

Line Type & Weight:

Rod/ Reel:

Fish Caught (Species / Size / Qty):

Water Clarity:______ Depth______Temp________

Notes Observations:

____

____

____

____

____

____

____

____

____

____

____

____

____

Fishing Log #37

Date:

Time:

Weather:

Location/Pond:

Lure Used:

Color/ Size:

Presentation (Wacky, Ned, Texas, etc.):

Line Type & Weight:

Rod/ Reel:

Fish Caught (Species / Size / Qty):

Water Clarity:______ Depth______Temp________

Notes Observations:

____

____

____

____

____

____

____

____

____

____

____

____

____

____

Fishing Log #38

Date:

Time:

Weather:

Location/Pond:

Lure Used:

Color/ Size:

Presentation (Wacky, Ned, Texas, etc.):

Line Type & Weight:

Rod/ Reel:

Fish Caught (Species / Size / Qty):

Water Clarity:_____ Depth_____Temp_______

Notes Observations:

____

____

____

____

____

____

____

____

____

____

____

____

Fishing Log #39

Date:

Time:

Weather:

Location/Pond:

Lure Used:

Color/ Size:

Presentation (Wacky, Ned, Texas, etc.):

Line Type & Weight:

Rod/ Reel:

Fish Caught (Species / Size / Qty):

Water Clarity:______ Depth______Temp________

Notes Observations:

____

____

____

____

____

____

____

____

____

____

____

____

____

Fishing Log #40

Date:

Time:

Weather:

Location/Pond:

Lure Used:

Color/ Size:

Presentation (Wacky, Ned, Texas, etc.):

Line Type & Weight:

Rod/ Reel:

Fish Caught (Species / Size / Qty):

Water Clarity:______ Depth______Temp________

Notes Observations:

____

____

____

____

____

____

____

____

____

____

____

____

____

____

Fishing Log #41

Date:

Time:

Weather:

Location/Pond:

Lure Used:

Color/ Size:

Presentation (Wacky, Ned, Texas, etc.):

Line Type & Weight:

Rod/ Reel:

Fish Caught (Species / Size / Qty):

Water Clarity:_____ Depth_____Temp_______

Notes Observations:

____

____

____

____

____

____

____

____

____

____

____

____

Fishing Log #42

Date:

Time:

Weather:

Location/Pond:

Lure Used:

Color/ Size:

Presentation (Wacky, Ned, Texas, etc.):

Line Type & Weight:

Rod/ Reel:

Fish Caught (Species / Size / Qty):

Water Clarity:______ Depth______Temp________

Notes Observations:

____
____
____
____
____
____
____
____
____
____
____
____
____
____

Fishing Log #43

Date:

Time:

Weather:

Location/Pond:

Lure Used:

Color/ Size:

Presentation (Wacky, Ned, Texas, etc.):

Line Type & Weight:

Rod/ Reel:

Fish Caught (Species / Size / Qty):

Water Clarity:______ Depth______Temp________

Notes Observations:

____

____

____

____

____

____

____

____

____

____

____

____

Fishing Log #44

Date:

Time:

Weather:

Location/Pond:

Lure Used:

Color/ Size:

Presentation (Wacky, Ned, Texas, etc.):

Line Type & Weight:

Rod/ Reel:

Fish Caught (Species / Size / Qty):

Water Clarity:______ Depth______Temp________

Notes Observations:

____
____
____
____
____
____
____
____
____
____
____
____
____

Fishing Log #45

Date:

Time:

Weather:

Location/Pond:

Lure Used:

Color/ Size:

Presentation (Wacky, Ned, Texas, etc.):

Line Type & Weight:

Rod/ Reel:

Fish Caught (Species / Size / Qty):

Water Clarity:______ Depth______Temp________

Notes Observations:

____
____
____
____
____
____
____
____
____
____
____
____

Fishing Log #46

Date:

Time:

Weather:

Location/Pond:

Lure Used:

Color/ Size:

Presentation (Wacky, Ned, Texas, etc.):

Line Type & Weight:

Rod/ Reel:

Fish Caught (Species / Size / Qty):

Water Clarity:______ Depth______Temp________

Notes Observations:

____
____
____
____
____
____
____
____
____
____
____
____
____

Fishing Log #47

Date:

Time:

Weather:

Location/Pond:

Lure Used:

Color/ Size:

Presentation (Wacky, Ned, Texas, etc.):

Line Type & Weight:

Rod/ Reel:

Fish Caught (Species / Size / Qty):

Water Clarity:_____ Depth_____Temp_______

Notes Observations:

____

____

____

____

____

____

____

____

____

____

____

____

____

Fishing Log #48

Date:

Time:

Weather:

Location/Pond:

Lure Used:

Color/ Size:

Presentation (Wacky, Ned, Texas, etc.):

Line Type & Weight:

Rod/ Reel:

Fish Caught (Species / Size / Qty):

Water Clarity:______ Depth______Temp________

Notes Observations:

____
____
____
____
____
____
____
____
____
____
____
____

Fishing Log #49

Date:

Time:

Weather:

Location/Pond:

Lure Used:

Color/ Size:

Presentation (Wacky, Ned, Texas, etc.):

Line Type & Weight:

Rod/ Reel:

Fish Caught (Species / Size / Qty):

Water Clarity:______ Depth______Temp________

Notes Observations:

____

____

____

____

____

____

____

____

____

____

____

____

____

Fishing Log #50

Date:

Time:

Weather:

Location/Pond:

Lure Used:

Color/ Size:

Presentation (Wacky, Ned, Texas, etc.):

Line Type & Weight:

Rod/ Reel:

Fish Caught (Species / Size / Qty):

Water Clarity:_____ Depth_____Temp_______

Notes Observations:

____
____
____
____
____
____
____
____
____
____
____
____
____

Best Fishing Trips				
Date	Lake/Pond	Total Catch/Species	Weight/Length	Rating

www.ingramcontent.com/pod-product-compliance
Lightning Source LLC
Chambersburg PA
CBHW071200300726
48975CB00004B/1228